Minnie and Moo
Go Dancing

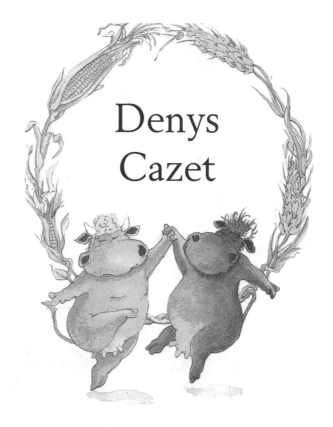

Denys
Cazet

SCHOLASTIC INC.
New York   Toronto   London   Auckland   Sydney
New Delhi   Hong Kong

D0964749

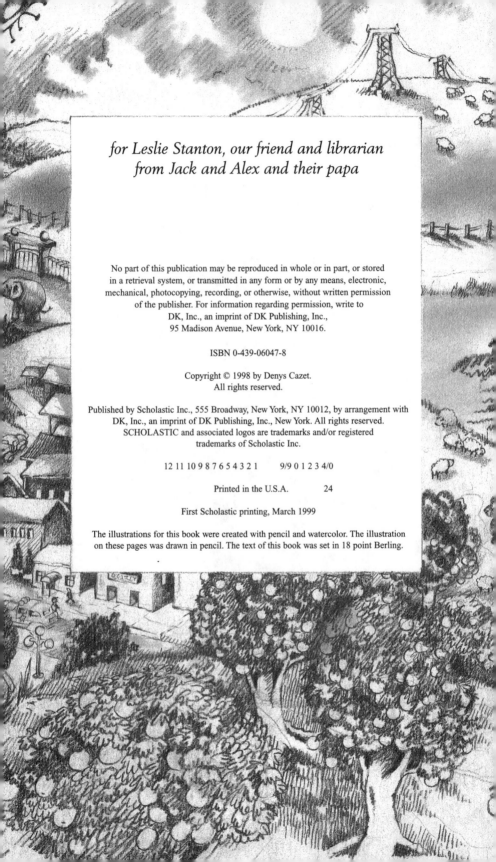

*for Leslie Stanton, our friend and librarian
from Jack and Alex and their papa*

ISBN 0-439-06047-8

Published by Scholastic Inc., 555 Broadway, New York, NY 10012, by arrangement with
DK, Inc., an imprint of DK Publishing, Inc., New York. All rights reserved.
SCHOLASTIC and associated logos are trademarks and/or registered
trademarks of Scholastic Inc.

12 11 10 9 8 7 6 5 4 3 2 1   9/9 0 1 2 3 4/0

Printed in the U.S.A.   24

First Scholastic printing, March 1999

The illustrations for this book were created with pencil and watercolor. The illustration
on these pages was drawn in pencil. The text of this book was set in 18 point Berling.

The First Wish

A soft wind settled in the trees.

Minnie and Moo sat quietly.

The sky turned pink.

It turned orange and red.

And then the sun was gone.

Minnie clapped.

"Lovely," she said. "Just lovely."

"Ummm?" said Moo.

"That was the best sunset
of the summer.

I'm going to give it a ten!"
said Minnie.

She wrote *10* on her scorecard.

"What did you give it, Moo?"

"What?" Moo said.

"Your score! Tonight's sunset!"

"Sunset?" said Moo.

Minnie sighed.

She put her scorecard down.

"Moo, are you thinking again?"

"A small think," said Moo.

She looked into the twilight.

"I was thinking . . ."

"Oh!" said Minnie.

"There's the first star.

Let's make a wish, Moo.

You first."

Moo closed her eyes.

"Thumbs," she said.

"I wish for a nice pair of thumbs."

The Second Wish

"Thumbs?" Minnie said.

Moo nodded.

"Yes," she said. "Thumbs."

She looked at the farmer's house.

Bright lights lit up the night.

People laughed.

They danced to music.

"We are only cows," said Moo sadly.

"Without thumbs . . .

we will never dance."

Minnie put her arm around Moo.

"Moo," she said.

"You don't need thumbs to dance.

It is true people have thumbs.

With thumbs,

people can make things.

But . . . can they make happiness?"

Moo thought about it.

"We have friends," Minnie said.

"We have a warm barn in winter.

We sleep under the stars

in the summer.

And we get milked every day!"

". . . with thumbs," added Moo.

11

Minnie and Moo sat quietly.

A second star appeared.

"I just made my wish," said Minnie.

"Come on, Moo. Let's go!"

"Where are we going?"

"Dancing!" said Minnie.

Magic

Minnie and Moo

slipped into the barn.

"Bea," Minnie called softly.

"Oh, Bea? Madge, where are you?"

No one answered.

"That's strange," said Moo.

"They're always here," said Minnie.
"Bea was the one
who told me about . . . THIS!"
"What?"

She pulled out a purple prom dress.

She held it up to Moo.

"It's you!" said Minnie.

"It is beautiful," said Moo. "But . . ."

Minnie smiled.

"We're going to a party," she said,

"and we don't need thumbs!"

"Hurry," said Moo.

"I know how all of this goes on.

I saw it in a magazine once!"

Minnie and Moo squeezed

into their dresses.

"This girdle thing

goes on the outside," said Moo.

"Yum," said Minnie. "Smell this, Moo."

"You spray that under your arms,"

said Moo. "And this, this is hair color.

What do you like best?

Red or green?"

"Red," said Minnie.

"Now for some lipstick," said Moo.

"And we are ready!"

Moo hugged Minnie.

"Oh, Minnie," she said.

"Good friends are such magic!"

The Party

Moo rang the doorbell.

"I'm so nervous," she said.

"Me too!" said Minnie.

"Hang on to your purse."

The door opened.

"HOLY COW!"

"It's Opal and Ruby!

John's twin sisters

from California!"

shouted the farmer's wife.

"Come on in," she said.

"Call me Poopsie. Everybody does."

Minnie and Moo followed her.

"You look just like your pictures,"

Poopsie said.

"John will be so happy.

What a perfect birthday surprise."

They went into the backyard.

"YOO-HOO!

Hank DePew! Bobo DePew!

Come over here

and meet someone!" yelled Poopsie.

"They're not married," she whispered.

Hank and Bobo waved.

They snapped their suspenders.

"Howdy," said Bobo.

"Howdy," said Hank.

"Wanna dance?"

Doing the Moo

"Grab your partners!"

called the fiddler.

Hank grabbed Minnie.

"YA-HOO!" he shouted.

Bobo grabbed Moo.

"YA-HOO!" he shouted.

Poopsie waved at them.

"Aren't they something!" she said.

"I used to have

a dress like that!

Come to think of it . . .

I had a dress like that one, too!"

Of course, I wore my girdle

on the inside."

The band played faster.

Moo danced faster.

She wiggled her hips.

She kicked, she spun.

She did a double-dip twist.

"What are we doing?"
whispered Minnie.

"We're doing the Moo," sang Moo.

"This girdle thing is killing me,"
Minnie panted.

"Get rid of it!" said Moo.

Minnie threw the girdle into the air.

"YA-HOO!" shouted Hank.

"YA-HOO!" shouted Bobo.

Hamburger

Moo plopped into a chair.

Minnie wheezed.

"I AM IN LOVE!" shouted Bobo.

"You gals sure know
how to hoof it!" said Hank.

"Try these burgers," said Bobo.

"We'll be right back," said Hank.

Minnie stared at the hamburgers.

"Yum!" said Moo. "This is tasty!"

Minnie gasped. "Moo . . ."

"Take a bite," said Moo.

"Moo . . ." Minnie said softly.

"Put it down."

"What?"

"Use your brain,"

said Minnie, tapping her head.

"Hamburgers are beef!

Oh, Moo. Didn't you know?

We are beef!

Moo . . . you're eating someone!"

Moo dropped her plate.

She stared at Minnie.

"Someone we knew?"

Minnie nodded.

"We found the Holsteins," she said.

"Oh, my!" cried Moo.

"I've eaten Madge."

"We could be next on the grill.

Run for it!" said Minnie. "Run!"

Moo grabbed

the platter of hamburgers.

"I've got the Holsteins," she said.

Ghosts

Minnie and Moo

rested under the old oak tree.

They hung the clothes on a branch.

Sadly, they buried the hamburgers.

Minnie put a marker on the grave.

"I'm sorry, Madge," Moo said.

"I didn't know it was you."

Minnie put her arm around Moo.

"You couldn't have known,"

said Minnie.

"Maybe it was Bea."

38

Minnie and Moo stood quietly.

"Something's coming."

"Ghosts?" said Minnie.

"Oh!" Moo said. "Hamburger ghosts!"

"They're getting closer!" Minnie gasped.

Suddenly, Bea and Madge Holstein
crashed into Minnie and Moo.
"OH!" shouted Bea and Madge.
"OH!" shouted Minnie and Moo.

"GHOSTS!" shouted Minnie.

"WHERE?" shouted Bea.

"YOU!" shouted Moo.

"US?" said Madge. "US?"

"Pinch me," said Bea. "Go on!"

Moo pinched Bea.

"OUCH!" Bea yelled. "See!"

"You don't feel like a ghost," said Moo.

"We were going to sleep under the stars,"

said Madge. "But we heard scary voices."

Bea pointed into the night. "Listen!"

"OPAL, RUBY, COME BACK!"

"Come on, Bea," said Madge.

"Hurry! Let's go back to the barn."

"OPAL, RUBY, WHERE ARE YOU?"

"Those are not ghosts!" said Minnie.

"OPAL, RUBY, COME BACK!"

"Run!" yelled Moo.

The Last Wish

"There!" shouted Hank.

"In that tree!" shouted Bobo.

Everyone ran to the old oak tree.

Poopsie pulled down the clothes.

"They're gone," she said.

"Without clothes?" said the farmer.

"YA-HOO," cried Hank and Bobo.

"Let's go back to the party,"
said the farmer.

"But John . . . your sisters . . ."

"Poopsie, they are not my sisters!

My sisters are ninety years old!"

"Goodness," said Poopsie.

Minnie peeked over the hill.

"Are they going?" Moo whispered.

"Yes," said Minnie.

Minnie and Moo sat quietly.

They listened to the music

as the light of the moon

filled the summer night.

After a while, Minnie stood up.

"May I have this dance?"

Moo stood and bowed.

"Thank you," said Moo.

Together,

they danced under the stars.

Opal and Ruby.

Minnie and Moo.